LATIN AMERICAN WOMEN WRITERS
Series Editors

Jean Franco, *Columbia University*

Francine Masiello, *University of California at Berkeley*

Tununa Mercado

Mary Louise Pratt, *Stanford University*

UNIVERSITY OF NEBRASKA PRESS • LINCOLN AND LONDON

Microfictions
Ana María Shua

Translated by Steven J. Stewart

Publication of this book was
assisted by a grant from the
National Endowment for the Arts.
"A great nation deserves great art."

Library of Congress
Cataloging-in-Publication Data

Shua, Ana María, 1951–
[Short stories. Selections. English]
Microfictions / Ana María Shua ; translated by
Steven J. Stewart.
p. cm. — (Latin American women writers)
The microfictions being presented in this
volume are taken from four previously
published Spanish-language books.
ISBN 978-0-8032-1376-0 (cloth : alk. paper) —
ISBN 978-0-8032-2090-4 (pbk. : alk. paper)
I. Stewart, Steven J., 1973– II. Title.
PQ7798.29.H8A6 2009
863'.64—dc22
2008039003

Set in Micro Extended and Frutiger by Kim Essman.
Designed by R. W. Boeche.

When a man rides a long time through wild regions he feels the desire for a city. Finally he comes to Isidora, a city where the buildings have spiral staircases encrusted with spiral sea-shells, where perfect telescopes and violins are made, where the foreigner hesitating between two women always encounters a third, where cockfights degenerate into bloody brawls among the bettors. He was thinking of all these things when he desired a city. Isidora, therefore, is the city of his dreams: with one difference. The dreamed-of city contained him as a young man; he arrives at Isidora in his old age. In the square there is the wall where the old men sit and watch the young go by; he is seated in a row with them. Desires are already memories.

Italo Calvino, from *Invisible Cities*

Contents

Acknowledgments

Thanks to the first publishers of these stories: "Peeling Carrots," "Portuguese Sauce," and "Fried Eggs" originally appeared in *Alimentum* 6 (2008). "Moment of Pleasure," "Reassuring" (as "Calming"), and "Foreseeing Everything" originally appeared in *Hanging Loose* 89 (Fall 2006). "Rumor in the Court" originally appeared in *Quick Fiction* 10 (Fall 2006). The epigraph is from *Invisible Cities* by Italo Calvino, trans. William Weaver (New York: Harcourt, 1974).

1

Monsters

Night Sounds

In the summer night, calm and warm, all that can be heard
is my sleeping daughter's breathing and the soft purring of
a refrigerator in heat calling for its mate.

Being a Rabbit

All day long I'm a rabbit, and it's only at night that I recover my human form. So why did I knit you these pajamas, complains my grandma, caressing the large and useless striped earflaps.

Hair Dryer

Let's say you're with a hair dryer. Let's say the dryer loves you. Let's say that it wants to take control of your body through persuasion or violence. Let's say that it's blowing warm air over your left ear, perhaps the more sensitive one. Let's say that you could unplug it if you wanted, if you thought of doing so. Then, let's shut up.

Matches

Matches are nothing like ants. Their ways are flickery and nocturnal, hardly gregarious, and they refuse to be part of a collective society in which every member's life is of little importance. Every time one lights up, it's an individual personality that goes out. They will only accept you if you're willing to have your head explode in an instant that's absolute, orgasmic, final, whose presumed ecstasy it's impossible to be sure of beforehand.

Flattery

This isn't the work of a human being, says the gentleman in the frock coat, looking closely at the deep and bloody marks left buried in the flesh. Come on, what a flatterer, you're exaggerating, I tell him, modest, my claws buried in my pockets.

She Covers Your Eyes

She covers your eyes and asks, who am I? She has the hands and voice of your youngest daughter. And now she wants your eyes.

Werewolf

With a ferocious grimace, gushing blood and spittle, the werewolf opens his jaws and bares his yellow fangs. A curious buzzing perforates the air. The werewolf is afraid. So is the dentist.

The Dead

Certain characters have boasted of visiting the world of the dead. I don't need to demonstrate that this is impossible: the dead don't all live together. On the other hand, there exists an intermediary world where our own dead visit us. To call to them is useless. They come and see us when they want and, what's worse, how they want.

Specters

If ghosts tremble in their sheets and hide from you, if skel-etons jump and take cover in their own tombs, don't brag about it, friend. Never brag about scaring specters. Their terrified expressions as they get out of your way are noth-ing more than ploys they use to try to make you believe you're still alive.

Spirits

You are strongly discouraged from having carnal relations with evil spirits. You are permitted, however, to invite them to have a cup of coffee after dinner, to go with them to the movies and eat pizza, to converse, finally, about how the weather was for their journey. You might object that such commonplace entertainments don't justify the trouble of invoking or creating them. And yet, how much we still have to learn from their exquisite manners.

The Party

Inside the storm door there's a clothes rack. There, the guests are asked to leave their bodies, which immediately acquire a pale hue. Though this precaution is efficient in fulfilling its designated function, that of helping the hostess and her servants save time cleaning up after the party, perhaps it's not a good idea. Many of the visitors are distracted while participating in the spiritual diversions prepared for them because they're afraid that someone might steal their most prized features (their dimples, their ankles, a certain agreeable relation between the widths of their shoulders and hips). Others would prefer to eat hors d'oeuvres. The majority, worried about conserving their perishable containers, leave too early. Not to mention those who prefer not to come, to miss out on the party.

Cousin and Grandmother

Cousin Nora is pregnant. It's good news, which the family had waited for with little patience. I ask grandmother if she's happy. She gives a distant smile, from the mist. So it was true, she tells me, happy: so it wasn't just a dream. But the mist is vast, it's dense, and my grandmother's eyes frighten me.

Voracious Baby

Every once in a while, almost unintentionally, the baby bites
the nipple. Afterward it keeps nursing. The mother lets out
a brief cry but immediately recovers her calm. During the
day, though progressively more pale and debilitated, mama
misses that fat and rosy baby that only comes at night, that
goes crawling off through the garden a little before dawn.

Kammapa, the Swallowing Monster

A Bantu legend describes (or perhaps doesn't describe) an amorphous monster named Khodumodumo (though some call it Kammapa). This being starts out by eating up a person who dares enter his realms; he later devours the warriors that go to rescue the first victims and advances on the village, swallowing everything in his path. Kammapa makes everything disappear into his limitless belly: trees, goats, chickens, houses, fields, people, and also the sun and moon. The earth is left shapeless and empty.

A small child—in some versions it's the pregnant woman who will give birth to him—is saved by hiding in the ash. Magically made into an adult in an instant, the child opens up Kammapa's belly with his sword and a shriek answers him: without meaning to, he has cut off the leg of one of the men inside. So he saves his people and restores the universe's form, but he gains a maimed enemy who has sworn eternal vengeance.

This story isn't impossible: I myself have a small scar on my face caused by the scalpel that cut open my mother's uterus.

Having Grown

How big you've gotten, says my aunt Rachel, with some ef-
fort, pressed against her bedroom wall with such force that
she can hardly introduce into her lungs the air she used in
marveling at the size of my hand that is trying, between the
index finger and thumb, to take her by the waist and bring
her closer to my ear.

Squids

Squids don't terrify me. As a sign of friendship, I braid and unbraid their tentacles. After all, I'm almost one of them: I too know how to hide myself in clouds of ink.

If Thy Right Hand Offend Thee

Because my right hand offended me, I cut it off and cast it aside. It walks all smug on its five little feet through the house and, what's even worse, keeps on offending me.

Treachery

Together the two of them immobilize my legs. Their touch burns me. Afterward they twist up my arms. They cover my face until I can't breathe. I've made up my mind this time: I'll never buy polyester sheets again. They really are treacherous.

Objects

Objects aren't always threatening. Sometimes they're even friendly. Sunday mornings, without going any farther, the nightstand brings me breakfast in bed.

Birth

I held still with the thermometer under my armpit for several hours, until I began to feel the first movements. Finally, I softly lifted my arm to remove the remains of the broken bulb and let the little thermometers crawl up my shoulder. I inclined my head toward them: in their sweet mercuric baby talk they said "mama."

True to Herself

Just look at you, it's incredible, you haven't changed a bit,
he flatters me, an old friend: exactly like you were years ago.
I bawl with pleasure and vanity and, in the arms of my exhausted wet nurse, keep on sucking.

If Only

They sprout up from the corners, from their tiny burrows.
They are weak and disgusting, dark and numerous. They
have antennae. They eat my food. If only they were cock-
roaches.

Warning

Above all, keep away from insects belonging to oriental warriors. There's nothing more dangerous, for example, than a centipede trained in the martial art of the flying kick.

Shooting Butterflies

I shoot down butterflies with a slingshot. The butterflies don't die. Wounded, crying, they drag themselves to my vicinity. I crush their heads with my heel. Even like that, destroyed, they attempt broken flights that only serve to splash me with blood and other semiliquid substances. Unexpectedly they reanimate: with claws bared and smashed heads dangling from their necks, they fling themselves at me. And how far away my four desperate little legs would carry me if some dolt hadn't nailed my tail to a tree trunk.

Fried Eggs

I have nothing against fried eggs. They're the ones who look at me with amazement, terrified, wide-eyed.

Cut!

The matchbox opens up all by itself. Two matches come out.
They greedily eat the pizza left on the table. When finished,
they devour each other until there's nothing left. Other vo-
racious matches come out of the box and head straight for
a bystander. They start on his feet. Cut! shouts the director.
But by now no one's paying attention.

Dolls

I vigilantly open my bedroom door trying to catch my dolls talking to each other. They, however, are silent, naked, serene. Their motionlessness doesn't surprise me, but it does reassure me. They've been dead for two days now.

Afterward

So now what do you think of me, I remark, while I slowly put my clothes back on. And even though it doesn't answer me, I know all too well how to interpret the ironic smile on the enormous, toothless mouth of my bathtub.

The Masks

In accordance with the strictest traditions, twelve midnight is the time to remove the masks. And nevertheless it's almost morning, the ball has ended, and I'm still here, in this mirrorless room, taking off the masks, the masks, the masks.

Advisors

More than one general in this world has gotten advice from his horse. General Quiroga's mount, for example, was a good adviser. Its recommendations, though not infallible, were much more humane than those of any armored tank consulted in the present.

Frustrated Vocation

A young man's vocation was to be a tree, but his family didn't permit him to develop his obvious aptitudes for branching out and even made him marry against his will. A whole life of frustration resulted in a horrible old age: he grew stiff and thin, he grew rigid and dry to the extreme point of becoming a television antenna. This legend gives us an explanation of the origin of television antennas, but not of their extravagant proliferation.

The Oak Tamer

A trained oak tree is a spectacle worth seeing. Some are capable of solving simple mathematical problems (adding and subtracting), though many people believe it's a trick. There was once a tamer who exhibited his tree circling the track on a skateboard, causing damage to the orchestra seats and panic among the children. At that point the circus director attacked the tree with a hatchet, but apparently the calamity was an excuse, apparently there was something going on between this solitary giant of the woods and the director's wife. The tamer collected his insurance money and never said a word.

Legal Problems for Ivies

A woman turns into ivy. She grows slowly, covering the exterior walls and roof of the house. Her heirs try to exercise their rights. They get a lawyer, go to court, put together proceedings. Nevertheless, it's impossible to certify the death. The ivy attends the meetings with its roots wrapped up in moist cotton, shows its proper ID, responds courteously to the questions of the judge who is (clearly) afraid of it. One of the grandsons decides to try some pruning shears. As the plant is cut from its roots, the walls of the house collapse, as the ivy was the only thing sustaining them. Unfortunately, the land isn't worth much.

The Head

A man comes in carrying a human head in his hand. The eyes of the head move, its mouth opens, it weakly complains. It makes for an uncomfortable situation. The littlest ones get scared. The bigger ones say that it's just an artificial head, a toy. They work out explanations: if this head stops (there, see?), then all you have to do is replace the batteries so that it works again. If this man stops (there, see?) and doesn't work anymore, then all you have to do is replace him with another. At which point several men enter and take away the head and the dead body.

Bad Manners

If your chicken champignon takes off, leaving a trail of sauce on the tablecloth in its wake, don't blame your guests. You can't expect such an exquisite dish to tolerate your table manners.

Role Change

In the beginning they made our ankles itch. We sought relief from the itching and swelling with toothpaste, potato peels, and cucumbers. Afterward they grew. For a while it was possible to employ them as beasts of burden. It's now claimed that our daily activities, even the most routine ones, cause them unbearable stinging. As their size exceeds that of our conception of the cosmos, it becomes impossible to prove the existence of such itching.

Hunger

When a bus has devoured more men and women than its bowels can agreeably accept, its digestive process is abruptly interrupted. The convulsive banging of its stomach stops (for lack of space), the secretion of gastric juices comes to an end, and the passengers are excreted through the rear door practically intact. The secretary of transportation refuses to take responsibility for those who dare travel in an empty bus.

Grains of Sand

Grains of sand have no king. They act on impulse, disorganized, mobilized by lesser chiefs who are generally made of mica or mother-of-pearl. The wind, footprints, and the waves cause disturbances in their communications. A squall is enough to indefinitely separate two interlocutors. Their scientists are investigating a system of reproduction that would make prolonged contact between their sexes unnecessary. Hopefully they won't find one.

Acoustic Sponges

A seventeenth-century Dutch captain in Tierra del Fuego
sees or thinks he sees sponges capable of absorbing and ex-
pelling sound. This information is transmitted to me by the
actual voice of Captain Voosterloch, caught in the skeleton
of one of them. Afterward, sadly, it's not good for anything
but soaping up.

Confusing Trail

It's invisible but it leaves tracks. You can follow it by its tracks. At a crossroads the tracks split up. They're invisible but they leave tracks. You can follow them by their tracks. Only, at every crossroads the tracks split up again.

A Thousand Possibilities

When I was an adolescent, there unfolded before me, like
a fan, all of my options: I could become an airplane pilot or
a teacher, a housewife, writer, boxer, or oil derrick. As time
passed, with every choice, every turn in the road, the fan
closed up, pointing in a single direction, until converting into
a single fate, upright and lonely: definitely an oil derrick.

In Hiding

If a relative of yours tries to hide from your view by chang-ing into a coffee bean, you should act entirely as if he had really managed to fool you. Mixed in with the other beans, he is to be placed in the receptacle of the grinder. There are few relatives who allow themselves to be ground in this way, without letting their nature be known, out of sheer pride.

Peyote in the Garden

To test its hallucinogenic effects, concentrated peyote juice is used to water the garden. The marigolds, greatly affected, go crazy: in their delirium, they believe themselves to be sequoias. The gladiolas fall into a dangerous stupor, which approximates a vegetative state. The rest of the plants have hallucinations that are generous, positive, and infuse them with a complex sense of happiness. In the end, all these effects of the peyote are impossible to prove except for the acidic and convulsive vomiting of the carnivorous plants, caused by the bad taste of the insects that feed on the nectar.

Taking a Liking

A woman gets thrown onto the tracks. The train destroys her legs. Though there were no cameras at the station, the event is broadcast on television: the woman is interviewed in the hospital, a reporter makes comments about the young hooligans and the lack of security on the platforms.

The next day an old bag lady and a young teacher are hurled onto the tracks and don't survive. During the week there are various new attacks. One channel installs its cameras in the most crowded station. Now it's possible to observe the death or mutilation of the victims in greater detail and at the same moment it occurs. The chance for fame stimulates the actions of the hooligans.

But the public gets tired of the excessively repeated spectacle. At this time the majority of the people (except for some suicides) stay away from the tracks or choose other means of transportation; the police, for their part, are excessively present; and the problem could have been completely controlled, except for the fact that the train has acquired a taste: it gets off track, crashes, stalks, at any hour, in the plazas, around corners, in any bedroom in the city. (The insecurity applies to apartments high up in skyscrapers.)

Flesh We Are

All of this is due (I'm referring, simply, to everything) to the constant reproduction of certain wanton microorganisms, not lacking intelligence, those that are (by the ignorant) typically called atoms.

Parents Meeting

In the parents meeting of the school, they discuss diverse ways of executing the teacher. Romina's mom stirs her coffee with a finger that slowly dissolves in the cup. Back in my day, I remember with melancholy, they went for stoning, and the executioners were the students themselves. On the patio, like always, shouts are heard.

Woman and Horse

In a popular story of the Chamacoco (an indigenous people of the Argentine-Paraguayan Chaco), a woman has a horse for a lover and dies giving birth to a foal too big for her body. Today a caesarian section would have saved her. Thus science collaborates with evil, which nature punishes.

2

Dreams

Auguries

If you dream of a bear, you'll be disgraced. If you dream of radishes, you'll get rich. If you dream of precious stones, beware of brunettes. If you dream of earthworms, you may fall into a trap. If you dream of me, I'm sorry: I'm a real nightmare.

Heat

If the heat makes the walls of your room go soft like butter (and they even start to melt a little), don't turn on the air-conditioning. In any case, it's too late for you and you'd just be wasting electricity.

Children's Dreams

If your house is a maze and in each room there's **something** waiting for you, if the chalk drawings you scribbled on your bedroom wall come to life and in the living room your sister's head drips blood onto the green chair's fabric, if there are *things* playing with your plastic animals in the bathtub, don't worry, little one, they're only children's nightmares; you'll grow up, and afterward you'll get old, and afterward you won't have any more horrible dreams.

Chemistry of Dreams

High-voltage electrical impulses, chaotic and senseless, unleash waves of chemical products that invade our brain, unchaining the physiological mechanism of dreaming. We dream, then (a horrendous nightmare), that our brains are invaded by waves of chemical products unleashed by senseless and chaotic high-voltage electrical impulses.

Guilt

If in a dream a man commits adultery with another man's wife, the victimized husband has the right to dream up the worst punishments for the other. The adulteress, for her part, should be forgiven.

Darkness

To get lost in dense darkness isn't so bad. What's much worse is that fickle and black darkness capable of penetrating any crack. In our bodies we have enough openings to permit each night the constant infiltration that darkens our innards, covering our eyes from inside, making us swell with nothingness.

Fetal Dreams

The dreams of a fetus in its mother's womb have that gelatinous, amorphous quality of jellyfish. They ascend through
the umbilical cord until mixing with the mother's blood,
which normally eliminates them with the remains of her own
desires through her urine, sweat, and sadness.

Cold Water

Cold water on the face to erase the traces of sleep, to erase the remains of the nightmare. Cold water on the face that's now smooth and featureless: erased.

The Hospital

Donkeys, men, earthworms, enormous stones, and arma-
dillos are stacked in the hospital. What an embarrassment
for the government—this is nothing but a stinking mess.
There are no bandages, no cures, no nurses, no CT scanners,
no ambulances, no beds, no doctors, no laboratory, no
plasma, no syringes, no operating room, not everyone is
hurt, not everyone is sick, what an embarrassment, an embarrassment, it's possible this isn't even a hospital.

How Much?

How much for the tomatoes, Don Matías? I courteously ask the grocer. Those aren't tomatoes, he tells me, they're marsupials. How much for the marsupials, Don Matías? I ask again, always courteous. My name isn't Don Matías, he tells me, my name is Spencer Tracy. Thinking about it, I realize it's possible he's not even a grocer.

Sanctuary

A lion attacks an antelope herd and kills one of them. The antelope rapidly flee. Still running, they solicit my protection and advice. I open my balcony door up for them and let them huddle together in my living room, shaking, with their long horns vibrating like antennae. I use their dung to fertilize my flowerpots and their horns to make skeins of yarn. But the balcony door is still half open, and I know one day an enemy will breach it: a lion (the same or a different one), an epidemic, a tax collector.

In Dreams

A man is attacked. He fights back. He's gravely wounded and taken prisoner. This happens in dreams. For various consecutive nights the man is in agony. One night, death comes before waking. The man keeps playing, working, and falling in love while awake as if he were completely alive; but his nights are, from that point on, unremembered and empty. Many years later, the man also dies on this side of the universe, acceding to a death populated with strange dreams.

Waiting

Waiting for the arrival of the train in the middle of the field, in Sunday dress, conversing, sharing the contents of the baskets, without worrying about the absence of an embankment, of crossties, of tracks, with the blissful, quiet certainty that no absurd train will come by to break the sweetness of waiting.

My Daughter

All babies need to be fed, except my own daughter. Never eating anything, she grows wildly under the blanket. I'm your mother, I introduce myself, when I judge she's big enough to recognize me. Quite the opposite, she responds to me harshly. And since I'm too hungry to argue, I keep crying until she gives me her breast.

On My Flute

Sweetly playing an old melody on my flute, I attract three
earthworms that live in the rubber tree pot. Play something
by the Beatles, they ask me, respectful but wanting to dance.
Since I only know lullabies, all three fall asleep on the floor.
Before waking up, I put them back in the pot and tuck them
in with loose dirt.

Being Pulled Out

A magician pulls a rabbit out of a hat. I am the rabbit. I am the magician. I am also the hat. With his rough pulling, the magician hurts my ears. The rabbit doesn't want to come out of the hat at the right time. And my satin-lined interior isn't exactly hygienic. If only I were nothing but the act of being pulled out.

Waiting in Line

In the line the people get angry. Some rail against the government and others against anarchy. At his window the functionary sits impassively. Hey, that guy is asleep, an agitated bald man in front of me says. No sir, we're the ones who are asleep, a woman explains to him in a very soft voice (if you wake up, you lose your turn). Many hours later, I give my name at the window only to discover I'm in the wrong dream.

While I Sleep

While I sleep, an earthquake destroys the city. The buildings fall like castles made of dominoes. In the morning the spectacle is terrible. Since I don't like it, I go back to sleep. While I sleep, an invasion of termites devours just about everything. In the morning I find them on my sheet. Since I don't like it, I go back to sleep. While I sleep, the river swells so much I wake up wet. Since I don't like it, I go back to sleep. While I sleep, time speeds up. In the morning I find myself in another century. Since I'm curious, I get up and go for a walk.

The Rivers

I cross a river by walking on a bridge. I cross another river by swimming. I cross a third, on a boat. In the distance there's another river. This is a strange country, I tell my companion. Are there many more rivers? As many as you can cross without waking up, he says to me without a mouth.

Arguing Again

Arguing again with my mother and she's right. My words wound, they're violent, and she's right. I'm twisted with anguish while I shriek ever more ferociously, and she's right. I wake up, but it doesn't help any: she keeps on being my mother, all the time.

Peeling Carrots

I cut my finger peeling carrots. Drops of tar spring from the cut and stain the floorboards. Trying to clean it up, I make a hole in the floor. In the room below there's a university meeting. I'm among the professors. Looking up, I discover myself spying. That's what you get for peeling carrots, I tell myself, very angry.

The Disguise

Hidden underneath this disguise, I killed a close relative.
They won't catch me. I won't receive the punishment I de-
sire and fear. Nevertheless, I really loved him. Nevertheless,
I'm naked.

Those Clingy Catfish

What to do, my God, with so many clingy catfish, with the crazy things so willing to invade your bed, and not out of hunger, Lord, but rather looking for love, panting, their gills of open coral, enduring their thirst with the certainty that the dike has broken, that the wave is on its way, it's coming, now it's me who visits them in their element, the catfish, with an asphyxiating affection.

Mashed Potatoes

I love mashed potatoes. I slide happily down their white peaks and dig tunnels that take me straight from one edge of the plate to the other, far beyond the reach of the fork.

Sensitive

Sometimes, when I'm asleep I'm a turtle and, less often, I'm still one after waking, all day long. She's such a sensitive girl, say my friends; and they give me friendly pats on my shell, pretending not to notice it. The mirror, friendly and false, also offers me its help, and I myself could almost forget about it if the cowardly lettuces didn't shudder as I walked past.

With My Pillow

I discuss everything with my pillow because I trust its judgment. It listens to me quietly and responds wisely. The blanket butts into the conversation. (In the end, I always follow the advice of my foolish mattress.)

Underneath the Blanket

That creeping sensation that our two heads alone on the pillow generate, underneath the blanket, many legs, definitively, unpleasantly more than four.

Dummy

In his dreams the ventriloquist is a dummy. The dummy, for his part, dreams of the ventriloquist's wife.

Wake Up

Wake up, it's late, a strange man yells at me from the door-way. *You* wake up, it's about time already, I reply. But the stubborn jerk keeps dreaming me.

Reassuring

They try to reassure me: the scream that just frightened me came from my own mouth. As I can't look at my own mouth, I touch it with both hands, trying to feel in the lips' texture some imprint of the passage of such a shriek. I finally find traces of it in the trembling of the left corner of my mouth, in the rigidity of my tongue, in the frothy spittle dripping down my chin. How reassuring.

One Side and the Other

She moves around on the bed, lifts her arms to protect herself from something invisible, murmurs rapid-fire words I
can't quite understand; and even though I touch her, even
though I shout and shake her, she doesn't react, I'm left out,
she's still awake, on her side of the vigil, or she's asleep, perhaps, but, in any case, she's stopped dreaming of me.

Disturbed Sleep

With his fragile sleep disturbed, he gets up. He circles the
room, from one side to another, desperate. Over and over
he attacks the source of the noise, trying to eliminate it or
drive it away. Haggard, defeated, he drops at last and falls
asleep, dead to the world from his own exhaustion. How
fleeting your fragile sleep is, my poor mosquito. How quickly
I disturb it again with my insomniac footsteps.

Insomnia

I consult Hindu texts and university texts, poetic texts and medieval texts, pornographic texts and bound texts. I collate them, eliminate deadwood, avoid reiterations. I discover a total of 327 ways to combat insomnia. It's impossible to convey them: their description is so boring no one could stay awake past the first. (This is way #328.)

Power over Horror

A friend of mine told me that they amputated both of her son's arms so that he wouldn't hurt himself with them. The first image I had, with the arms cut off at the shoulders, was intolerable. Afterward I was able to think that they probably left him his elbow joints. I imagined prosthetic hands that had only the forefinger and thumb, and I wondered how the nerves could transmit impulses to such an apparatus.

During the night, I woke up many times and everything was the same. Only in the morning did I succeed in transforming the conversation with my friend into a dream. If only I had that power every morning.

Fishfoot

—There was a fish hurting my foot.

—Was it a shark eating you?

—It wasn't a shark, it didn't eat me, it wasn't biting me.

—But it hurt you.

—Yes. I was putting my foot in . . . There was water.
And it pulled down, hard. I couldn't see it.

—It was pulling your foot?

—It wasn't pulling my foot. It was hurting it. It was
pulling but not my foot. It was a very strange fish.

—What was it like?

—I didn't see it, but I knew it was a fish and I remember
the words very strange.

—And afterward?

—Afterward I'm here. Here, where is here?

3

Magic

Message

In the darkness the hands grip each other more tightly. The medium shakes in her seat. Her eyes grow intensely bright; incomprehensible sounds escape her lips. She finally manages to articulate her first words. "This is a recorded message," she begins in a monotonous metallic voice.

Errors

But be careful: a minuscule error in pronouncing the secret words (lengthening a vowel or an improper pause, the inadvertent gesture of scratching one's leg) can lead to frightening consequences. Like the growth of two large, floppy, fuzzy ears on the most comfortable chair of the house, in which no one will then dare sit. Like the brisk dropping of a neophyte spellcaster's pants in the presence of four hundred demons and a friend of his mother. Or the complete destruction of the world.

The Good-Luck Charm

The parents of a friend stole an ebony cat from a London store. They were detained, delayed, deported. Thanks to this incident, they missed a flight that exploded without taking off from Heathrow Airport. From then on, each time they leave Buenos Aires, they steal an ebony cat from a store a few days before returning.

As ebony cats are rare, they always carry one in their suitcases. Sometimes, it's very difficult to convince a store owner to buy it from them (even for pennies) and they are forced to give it to him. Afterward, when they steal it, it doesn't bring them so much luck.

Watching TV

How strange to be like this, on the sofa, watching my own face making clumsy faces on the screen. The show's not bad but my acting leaves a lot to be desired. I don't recognize my voice; and my gestures seem false, derivative, hardly spontaneous. And the strangest thing, perhaps, is that the show is live.

Sorcerer and Sultan

The sorcerer plunges the sultan's head into the magical waters of the pond, where he will be able to live and experience diverse wonders. The spell doesn't work and the sultan drowns. With the support of the palace guards, the sorcerer becomes sultan. The first decree of his government is to prohibit the entry of sorcerers into the realm.

The Keys of Fate

There are six keys of fate. The golden key is the key to misery. The silver one is the key to pain. That of Chinese copper is the key to death. The iron one is the key to power. The platinum one is the key to happiness and wisdom. The bronze key is the key to the garage.

Made Stupid by Pain

At the top of a tree, a woman holds open the trousers of her dead husband. The priest has told her that the man is in heaven, and she waits for him to fall at any moment. Poor fool, she should know better. Her husband falls from heaven once a day, but never on the same tree. There are others waiting for him as well.

Cannon

An excellent cannon, an incredibly powerful shot. Lamentably, the kick is just as strong. The cannonball would go all the way around the world if it didn't always collide with the cannon just a little bit this side of the antipodes.

Life and the Moon

Le-eyo was one of the first men, from whom the Masai descend. To let him conquer death, the demigod Naiteru-kop commanded him that when he disposed of the first corpse he must say the following: "Man, die and come back to life; moon, die and come back no more." A child died soon afterward, but, as it wasn't one of his own children, Le-eyo said to himself, "This child isn't mine; when I throw away the body I'll say, 'Man, die and come back no more; moon, die and come back to life.'"

But later on, when one of his own children died, it was useless to pronounce the magic words as he had been taught. The child didn't revive. For that reason, from then on, man dies and the moon is reborn.

Let us not hate Le-eyo. Who indeed would be capable of forever renouncing the moon for someone else's child?

The Curse

The old man dies cursing his assassin. No one knows what the curse consists of. The assassin lives with a constant sense of dread. A fortune-teller assures him that this daily fear *is* the curse. Until the day of his death, the assassin won't know that the fortune-teller was wrong. Afterward, it will be too late.

Juggling Show

As part of the show, the clown is juggling three oranges. Inside one of the pieces of fruit, a woman dressed in red and
gray is applying liquid eyeliner to her eyes with a small, old-
fashioned brush. Now, as always happens to her just when
she gets in a hurry, a drop of eyeliner gets into her left eye,
right by the tear duct. The eye turns red and burns, and she
can't rub it to keep the makeup from running. This scene
isn't part of the show, and it would be a shame for everyone if the orange were to fall.

Fortune-telling

I know that at the bottom of the cup, my fate is concealed in the coffee residue. To discover it, I drink for hours from the liquid hiding it, for days at a time. The liquid is dark, never ending. To drink it forever is my fate.

Telephone

Let's be realistic: a disembodied voice is all the telephone offers us. You need to have a lot of imagination and an excess of trust to always postulate a solid body on the other side emitting it.

Genie

I enthusiastically rub the lamp. The genie immediately appears, but he looks tired. I can make all of your dreams come true, he announces, using the standard phrase. How tranquilly I'd sleep if I could ask him for the opposite.

4

Health

Scientific Discussion

It's a virus, says one. It's clearly, evidently a bacterium, af-
firms another who is even more prestigious. Let's call it a
microorganism, proposes a third, trying to reach a consen-
sus. In any case, there's no doubt that it's a matter of a microorganism, small but well formed, with characteristics
capable of driving any scientist crazy. Right now it's doing
a strip tease.

Incubation

The world is cruel, my belly is warm: he doesn't want to be born and I understand. And nevertheless, how hard it is for me (though there's no sacrifice too great for a mother to bear) to keep this loving and rebellious teenager in my inordinately dilated womb now that he's secretly started smoking (a mother can always tell), causing little columns of smoke to come out of my belly button.

The Young Man
Destined to be My Grandfather

To avoid being sent to war, the young man destined to be my grandfather had all his teeth pulled out, but it didn't work. Then he cut off all the fingers of his right hand, but it wasn't enough. With an axe he amputated half a leg, but it still wasn't sufficient. He introduced a sharp object into his ear to make himself deaf, but he was still approved. In the end, he mutilated himself in such a way that he changed his destiny: they didn't send him to the war, but neither could he be my grandfather.

Bugs in the Fruit

I bite into a piece of fruit. The fruit has worms. The worms are contagious, my mom says. That's why I'm so itchy. I take off my shoes and stockings. I have white worms, wiggling, between my toes. If I remove them, more sprout. They're annoying but it's worth it: when my sister sees them, she'll never want to bite me again.

Natural Flowerpot

If you have the right shape to hold them and enough dirt for their roots, don't be surprised if begonias bloom in your belly button. Though it's recommended that you continue hiding them underneath baggy clothing, pretending to be worried about the excessive enlargement of your belly, you should be proud of them when you strip down in front of a woman: they are your begonias, unique, glorious, nontransferable, capable of driving crazy the most aloof of females, or at least it's good, sweetheart, that they think so.

Invaders

Let's admit that they are small and that there are many of them. Let's admit that they don't understand your language. Let's admit that you tried, desperately, to communicate with them through signs. Let's admit (and it doesn't take much) that your signs have another meaning in the gesticulative language of their culture. Even then they must know by now that nothing justifies their insistent presence in your bloodstream.

Identity and Alteration

If during your usual walk on this park's gravel path you happen to kick or involuntarily step on a small germ, don't
worry about the retaliation of its elders. Their extravagant
growth has made them no less indifferent to the cries of
their offspring.

What Was There

An ingenious set of video equipment, introduced rectally, explores the patient's bowels. Watching the screen, the doctor slowly grows pale. The patient, awake, sees the expression and understands everything. With no thought for the pain, he yanks out the long, flexible tube with the video camera and runs out half dressed.

The assistant and the nurse disappear or die over the course of the next week. The doctor is being held but refuses to make a statement, even when threatened, even when tortured.

Weight Watchers

In the group, we talked today about the need for relaxing. Stress, the coordinator explained to us, leads to temptation.

"I know various relaxation techniques," offered one member. "The simplest consists of imagining that your body is populated by dwarves that work without rest. When the day's work is done, the first ones to withdraw are the dwarves working in your feet. Exhausted, they drop their tools and slowly leave your body. Afterward you should continue with your legs."

When the woman stopped talking and stood to leave, no one expected to see a tiny hammer, computer, or pick drop from her skirt. We all had thought that the dwarves were only a metaphor.

Which is precisely how the giants in whose bodies we labor without rest must look at it.

A Bad Ankle Sprain

A married woman, forty-five years old, mother of three daughters, complained for months about sharp pains in her right ankle. One day she let loose a shriek that pierced the air. Her ankle had been transformed into an itinerant Buddhist priest who was no longer willing to function as a joint. Her foot, which was no longer connected to the rest of the leg, took off. The woman decided to purge her sins by following the priest through the world, but because of her limp she moved slowly and soon fell behind. Years later, after the woman had been forgotten, one of the house servants discovered the disappearance of some food from the kitchen due not to a mouse but to a wild foot living in a hole in the garden.

Misfortunes Hung Out to Dry

One night, poor thieves steal the clothes I've hung out to dry. The next night, I hang out my (well-wrung) misfortunes, made wet by grief. The next morning, I'm definitively happy.

Erotic Appetites

Very little has been written about the erotic appetites of certain microorganisms. As if everything for them were a matter a reproducing, as if those ferocious dances didn't exist, the out-of-proportion courting, the slow stripping of membranes culminating in the fusion of cytoplasms, the wild vibration of the columns of DNA twisting and untwisting in a tiny but fevered joy, with the cilia let loose in the violent liquid agar, causing, in the end, the hand to tremble, the hand of whoever tries to describe or capture their frenzy, confounding her axon-dendritic connections so that very little continues to be written about their erotic appetites, very little.

Memory Loss

To hide the fact that he doesn't remember them, he avoids saying names. To hide the fact that he doesn't recognize faces, he treats everyone like a close friend. He constantly watches others, imitating their expressions and actions with a second's delay. His world is fragile, strange, and desolate; but it nevertheless does have some compensations. No one else can have a different woman each night by having the one he's been married to for (according to her) twenty years.

Entering Someone Else's Body

It's possible to get into someone else's body through inges-
tion or surgery or possession or sex. Those who want to get
out would do well to make sure they have a scalpel before
going in. Some surgeons always carry one.

Femur

They operated on my grandpa. They took out the head of his femur, which had broken, and they put in a platinum screw. My dad was left with the femur head, as a souvenir. It wandered around the house until my mom threw it out because it smelled bad. When my grandpa dies, I want the platinum screw.

Game Show

It's a television game show. The children put on shoes of the brand sponsoring the program. Each mother has to recognize her child looking only at his or her little legs though a window of the set. The country is poor; the prizes matter. The participants get together and agree to always win. If some mother makes a mistake, she doesn't say so. Afterward, each takes home the child she has chosen, even if it's not the same one she brought. It's necessary to keep the charade up for a long time since the company controls the social workers who visit the contestants' homes. Some children lose out, but others come out ahead. It's also said that some mothers cheat, that they choose wrong on purpose.

Life or Death

The game is called Life or Death and the best part is operating on the patients. But since we don't know the instruc-
tions (we pirated the game instead of buying it), the sick
people always die on us. The game is fun but ends badly.
The same thing is going to happen to us. Playing it, we try
to forget.

Crime

The man raises the gun. For a second, his fate is uncertain. He looks around. He knows that not one of the objects surrounding him will change its shape or meaning when he becomes an assassin. The small act he's about to carry out will only change his own history and the history of his victim. He mercilessly observes the physical changes that terror imposes: the spasmodic trembling, the blacking out that makes the victim's lips turn pale and emphasizes the bags under his eyes. After that, he fires and falls, lightly splashing the mirror.

Unforeseen Interruption

Just once I dared to interrupt her, with such bad results, with such a frenetic and absurd reaction from my relatives, that I've decided to leave her alone to meet her natural end. So here I am, waiting for her to finish, once and for all, this long and boring death.

5

Literature

Wolf

With lilies, morning glory, and larkspur, I entertain myself in the woods. The lilies are soft, the morning glory is white, and the larkspur smells wonderful. But the hours pass by and the wolf doesn't come. What does my grandmother have that I don't?

Hare

While the nonchalant hare sleeps, the constant tortoise gets closer to the goal. What a stupid nightmare, says the hare, waking up in a bad mood. He stretches, gets up, and with three jumps wins the race.

Frog and Princess

This is the story of a prince transformed into a frog retransformed into a prince by the kiss of a princess whom he marries only to discover that she has—the gentle surprises of living together—the odd habit of catching flies with her long tongue, or the story of a frog transformed into a princess retransformed into a frog by being abandoned by an indignant, thankless prince; everything depends, finally, on whose side you're looking at.

Frog and Princess III

The princess kisses the frog, which is transformed into a prince; she kisses the prince, who changes into a washbasin; she kisses the washbasin, which turns into a petrel; she kisses the petrel, which takes the form of a heliotrope; she kisses the heliotrope, which turns into a mirror; and it's useless and even dangerous for the princess to insist on kissing her own image, but she does it, in any case, contentedly.

Frog and Princess IV

Emboldened by her initial success with the frog, the princess spends her days kissing burros, spiders, vultures, worms, wild boars, vipers, snails, and grooms, obtaining, it must be admitted, some occasional transformation (under the prince's jealous gaze): a wild boar that changes into a viper, some vulture that becomes a snail, and the always fresh hope of the grooms, who dream of being transformed into heirs of the throne.

Frog and Princess V

Considering the length and skill of his tongue, the princess wonders about her husband. Was he truly a prince before being a frog? Or was he really a frog, originally a frog, to which a fairy or similar being had granted the privilege of exchanging his amphibious lineage for humanity if he obtained the princely kiss? Her mind is gripped by such doubts during the exertions of giving birth, just before hearing the singular cries of her baby tadpole.

Cinderella III

Warned by their reading, Cinderella's stepsisters manage to modify, through expensive surgeries, the size of their feet, long before attending that famous ball. With three women fitting perfectly into the glass slipper, the prince decides to marry the one who comes with the biggest dowry. The new princess hires scribes who write the story as she dictates it.

In Glass Coffins

Lenin and Snow White in their respective glass coffins and that long line of charming princes, of tourists, that nevertheless doesn't manage to compensate for the frightening absence of dwarves.

Swans in the Lake

Ten swans arrive at the lake. Taking off their feathery out-fits, they are converted into ten naked young maidens. A bold youth steals one of the winged suits. Leaving the lake, the first of the young maidens discovers that her swan dis-guise has disappeared. Nevertheless, when the second maiden leaves the lake, she insists that the missing suit is hers and not her sister's. The third maiden leaves the lake and clam-ors for her winged clothing, refusing to put on any other. The fourth maiden insists that the remaining outfits belong to her sisters and that hers is the only dress that has been stolen. Ten shouting naked maidens angrily search the lake's shores. The bold youth tries to flee but it's too late.

Tarzan II

An ecological pioneer in his own way, Tarzan has always been a great defender of animals. But even so, he's put off by the approach of that white man named Francis who comes from Italy, the city of Assisi, who insists on calling them Brother Tantor, Sister Cheeta.

Sculpture

While the sculptor embraces her, trying to infuse her with his breath of life, the statue smiles impassively, somewhat amazed as she admires the perfection of the sculptor, her creation.

Plunge

Never plunge your head in for longer than the manuals rec-
ommend and certainly not with your eyes open. To live for
thirty years as a river nymph doesn't make up for the loss of
your existence as a human, and much less for that of your
contact lenses.

Like Ulysses

Like Ulysses, a man comes home from the war, or from jail, or from the wilderness. Twenty years have passed. His eyes are different. A blow has left his nose broken. Now he looks a little like Kirk Douglas, though his hair is sparse and almost white and the rags hang from his body in an ugly way. Everyone recognizes him perfectly well, but they hide it, except his stupid dog, who receives another one of those epic kicks.

Riddle

With my flesh chased, bitten, wounded by the acids secreted by this cursed stone stomach, my only pain is still not having found the answer to the mystery, the Enigma of which I myself will form part as soon as the Sphinx finishes digesting.

False Codex

Abate falsifies a codex whose antiquity is vouched for by eminent experts. The codex includes a chronicle of certain extraordinary acts in the past. Investigators discover new proofs (documents, objects, relations) that confirm the authenticity of the false chronicle. Before dying, Abate confesses to fraud; but it's too late, the past is now there, strong, weighty and verifiable like a dinosaur fossil—to modify it would provoke bloodbaths in the present; his confessor keeps the secret.

Ancient Japanese Story

In an ancient Japanese story a fox challenges a badger. Both are versed in the arts of transformation: they will take turns trying to fool each other.

At the side of the path, the badger, who is pious, sees a temple. Inside, there are various statues of the Buddha. When he's about to leave his offering, he notices a fox's tail showing from behind one of the statues. He pulls the tail, and the temple and statues go back to being a fox.

The fox continues walking down the path. He's interrupted by a prince's entourage. The army moves forward. A soldier pushes him off of the path. Following behind, on luxuriously saddled horses, are the courtesans, surrounding the litter of the prince, who is seen through brocaded curtains. A crowd of beggars comes behind, fighting for the pieces of copper and silver tossed out by the courtesans. The fox waits patiently. The last urchin has a badger's tail. When the tail is pulled, the whole entourage (army, courtesans, litter, prince, and beggars) turns back into a badger.

Then the fox turns into an ancient Japanese story and wins. The reader is invited to find the tail.

The Unflappable Man

To irritate an unflappable man, a bad poet skins a camel and
wears its skin inside out, with the hair inside and the flesh
and fat outside. Stinking and covered with flies, he knocks
on the mansion's door: the unflappable man has the door
opened. He sits down next to him and the unflappable man
bears the stink smiling. He touches him with a repugnant
leg and the unflappable man returns the caress. He ridicules
him with an epigram and the unflappable man laughs and
orders that he be given a bag of dinars. After that he insults
him and the unflappable man orders that he be given a hundred dinars more. The poet admits defeat and takes off his
disguise. To honor his host, he recites his complete works.
At which point the unflappable man orders that he be cut
up into very small pieces.

The Treasure Map

Two scoundrels sell a treasure map to a fool. The fool digs in the marked spot and finds nothing. The scoundrels bet the money at a casino and win a fortune.

The fool's wife leaves him and runs off with one of the scoundrels or perhaps both. The fool sits down by the door of his shack to lament the breaking down of traditional codes.

A Credible Story

John Aubrey writes that Thomas Traherne told of seeing a basket floating in the air and that the basket was a ghost. It's difficult to determine, no matter how often you reread the text, whether this is Aubrey's conclusion or Traherne's observation. What makes the ghostly effect believable is, in any case, a certain doubt on the part of the second narrator, who can't remember if the first narrator and protagonist of this story spoke or not of having also seen, in the floating basket, some fruit.

Rumor in the Court

It is said in the court of the czars that inside a bear of the forest of Y—— there's a fox; and if you kill that fox and try to skin it, you will see a duck come out of its belly; and inside of this duck, which is female, there's an egg; and if you break this egg, you will find a silver brooch in its yolk; and if you stick that silver brooch into the index finger of the czar's son, the empire will be destroyed and the court scattered and the czars will die and their elders and vassals and relatives will die. It's true that the forests of Y—— are fenced off and guarded, but there are many hunters, it is suspected that these include members of the guard itself, in any case it's October and it's cold.

Western

The men leave the saloon and face off on the dusty street, under the heavy sun. The younger and better-dressed one is defending the farmers and loves her. The older one, with a mustache, is fighting for the cattlemen and wants nothing but her. Her name is Loneliness, and she's the prettiest mare in the county. There's also a woman, but she's not important.

The Palmist

The palmist reads his own destiny in the hand of the one who will murder him. In my hand, however, he reads the complete works of Oscar Wilde. What an aptitude for synthesis, he admires. And he foretells for me a literary destiny.

Shipwreck

Lower the jib! orders the captain. Lower the jib! repeats the first mate. Luff starboard! shouts the captain. Luff starboard! repeats the first mate. Careful with the bowsprit! shouts the captain. The bowsprit! repeats the first mate. Take down the mizzenmast! shouts the captain. The mizzenmast! repeats the first mate. Meanwhile, the storm's getting worse and we sailors are running around the deck confused. If we can't find a dictionary soon, we're going to wreck for sure.

Like Everyone Else

I heard, like everyone else, the shouts asking for help. I ran, like everyone else, here. But now, watching the struggle, like everyone else, can I even decipher which is the victim and which is the attacker? I'll wait, like everyone else, for the show to end. Afterward, we'll hang up the corpse and we'll deliver the reward to the survivor. Like everyone else, like always.

Never Tell It Beforehand

A writer tells the idea for a story he's about to write. He tells it at a table in a café and it's a good idea, the air grows tense around his words, the story is tangible to the extent that the cigarette smoke doesn't cross through it, the smoke columns delineate its transparent contours. But afterward, when he tries to transform it into letters, he sees previously ignored cracks where the words flow, there are minefields, a mist of mediocrity invades the text, and the gods reject the offering of a victim that is no longer pure, that others before them have taken pleasure in.

Poetry Is You

Your presence and your voice invade everything, constantly; I don't listen to you but still hear you, that discordant sound converted into the music at the heart of my life, that compact mass of noises from which my mind occasionally makes some sense, in which I move with heaviness, like a diver weighed down by scores of atmospheres pressing his body against the depths of the sea. Perhaps that's why, my love, *I like you when you're quiet and it's almost like you're gone*.

Stones at Birds

Don't throw stones at birds because they might not be birds; they might not be stones; you might unintentionally be throwing oranges at helicopters, melons at bats, subway tokens at clouds; you might not even really be throwing but rather delivering, selling, blowing, or, what's even worse, exercising an intransitive verb.

Screenplay

In the original version the protagonist is a girl, very young, barely an adolescent, but it's realized that this puts a damper on possible conflicts, she's made to be twenty-five, she's blonde, married, until they subtly prefer that she be a man, a trickster type getting older by the day, a few logical expediencies convert him into a weak old man with cheeks that are rosy, bleary and immediately into a girl too smart for her own good. In the moment the girl is transformed into a dog, into that old German shepherd who, likeable and furry, will earn the public's applause, her cells explode across the table and scatter a gelatinous, burning substance that devours the bibliographical material, the cassettes, the screenplay writer himself, the producer's building and little by little the world, the galaxy, the universe itself, reduced to that minimal point, before the first heartbeat, a story that anyone could consider monotonous, anonymous, but which encapsulates all stories for that Ensemble of Olympian Spectators who applaud, Divinely fascinated.

6

Men and Women

Secret of Seduction

For some women, the heat of wax spilled over naked legs.
For others, the longest days (those of hunger), or the knife
that gives form to the rebellious flesh and molds the bones
of the face. For others, finally, the pain of being beautiful.
For her, what's enough is the rumor known to everyone, it's
enough that they know who she is, or, better said, whose
she is: for her, the neighbor's wife.

Love Triangle

A loves B, who loves C. As can easily be seen, B is pregnant.
Determine the sex of A and C, and enumerate all the possible combinations as to the sexual preferences in the vertices
of the ABC triangle, considering that love isn't necessary to
cause pregnancy and that in the alphabet there are so many
other letters, in the universe, so many disparate alphabets.

The Shaman's Power

While the Toba chief signed a peace treaty with the white men, his wife entertained another man. Taigoyic heard about it from the messenger birds. As he was a master of dog magic, he made it so that the guilty ones would be stuck together until he returned. Thus, when he returned to his hut, he found the man and woman in despair, half dead with hunger and thirst, naked and trapped, because their sexes had been stuck together for many days.

Others say they were faking it.

Foreseeing Everything

He traveled two hours on the four o'clock train, and now he's standing on the tree-lined street watching an automatic sprinkler rotate above the grass in an irregular and novel way, forming unexpected rainbows. Now he's going to the house to kill the woman, with the .22 caliber pistol he's carrying in his pocket wrapped in a handkerchief. It's not a powerful gun: he'll have to place it directly against her forehead or ear to be sure. But the summertime is sweet, and in the trembling of the water drops on the grass the man discovers he's no longer in love. The worst of it, what he hadn't counted on, is having to go back on that damned rush hour train.

Portuguese Sauce

A quarreling couple has guests over. There's chicken with Portuguese sauce. The wife serves the white meat to the male guest and offers him sauce. The husband is suspicious of his wife. With exaggerated courtesy, he offers sauce to the female guest. The wife is suspicious of her husband. She insists on adding sauce to the male guest's plate. The guests are highly suspicious of the chicken.

The Vengeful Knight

The clever maid knows that the knight hates and loves her. On the wedding night, she sets a life-size doll made of breadcrumbs in her place. A bladder filled with milk and honey takes the place of her heart.

The knight enters the shadowy room. He cries out for vengeance. With his dagger he pierces the heart of what he thinks is his beloved. A sweet, thick liquid splashes his face, his lips.

"How sweet was my love," he sobs in despair. "If only I could bring her back to life."

"Here I am," says the clever girl, emerging from underneath the bed.

"To kill her again and again," says the happy knight, thrusting in his dagger.

Afterward, the sobbing begins again.

Too Young

A man who is too young approaches a woman. He still doesn't know what he wants from her. Perhaps just this: To be close. To smell her scent. To look carefully at her hands, the filigree of her skin. To touch her. To eat, with a capricious sauce, a steak from her right buttock, cooked over a grill. Or to ask her to lend him some money.

Elephant Seals

Elephant seals dedicate themselves to mating for two months out of the year. They don't take any breaks, not even for eating, which is why they lose up to 30 percent of their body weight. On the Valdes Peninsula, a certain well-known specimen managed to build a harem of 104 females, pairing with each of them in the brief span of a season. The scientists who evaluated his performance observed that the pinniped mocked them by making crude gestures with its flippers in an obvious allusion to the absence of a penile bone (characteristic of its species) in the fragile anatomy of the human males.

Virgins

If paradise is fertile with virgins for a good Muslim male, what does it hold for an observant Muslim female? A harem of submissive men at her command would be worth less than nothing (less than a single sesame seed) compared to the glory of being the favorite in a harem of 100,432 beautiful women. (The other 100,431 are in hell.)

The White Queen

Grave danger for the White Queen. At the point of being burned in the bonfire, accused of practicing bestiality with the horses, of standing naked at the windows of the towers, of corrupting the peasants, of breaking the monastic calm of the bishops. Pardoned, however, and buried with honors for her great services to the state: sacrificing herself to the mortal embrace of the Black King, drawing him thereby into an ambush in which he himself falls, surprisingly happy at having finally disproved his impotence. (The White King's secret envy.)

The Last Coffee

The woman's hands were uselessly shredding the paper nap-
kin: this is the last time, she said, in a quiet voice. His hands
were dark and hairy and he was caressing one of her hands
atop the bar: this is the last time, he repeated. And though
both of them knew it was a lie, they looked at each other
with genuine anguish, because they also knew that emo-
tion stimulates desire; it establishes memories and justifies,
more than anything else, sadness.

Moment of Pleasure

Everything is set for pleasure, but pleasure doesn't come, the hour is late, it's slow in dressing for the party, it gets ambushed, the fringe of its tunic gets caught in the low branches, it's held up by an immigration official. Everything was set for pleasure and nevertheless, when pleasure shows up, the party's over. You have to understand, then, why they go to sleep like that, immediately, back to back, silent and frustrated.

House of Geishas

1. Plantation

A large and conveniently black man is in charge of making sure that the clients follow the rules of the House. The rhythmic pounding of his fists on the heads of the rule breakers can so much as bury them in the earth of the garden, especially if it's raining or has rained. From there comes the peculiar flora that surrounds the House in spring and the notable fruits of summer, those branches loaded with hands that are loose, curved, agitated by the wind, those flowers with an eye or a mouth in the corolla and you just have to see some of their smiles. Of those planted in the middle of winter, a high percentage don't grow right.

2. Secondary Benefits of Some Clients

When a client from Psseria departs, the woman's room is left crisscrossed from floor to ceiling and in all directions by fat threads, sticky, like thick spittle, that when dried turn into a powder highly valued as a condiment. Nevertheless, no woman likes to receive one.

3. Ghost Client I

The women tell each other stories of a ghost client, whose demanding ectoplasm would visit some (though not all), whose existence could be confirmed by Ermelinda's giving birth to an invisible child, one that she attributes, instead, to an official from the tax commission.

4. Classification

They classify the clients according to what they ask for, the clothes they wear, or the way they move their ears. Sometimes there are coincidences. For example, the majority of clients can't move their ears at all, but those who can wiggle their lobes tend to wear wide-brimmed hats and ask for absinthe and for Catalina.

5. Imitation

A small-town brothel that imitates a famous brothel of the capital that imitates the brothels of New Orleans that imitate the ideas that Americans have of the brothels of Paris. A small-town brothel, a distant copy: balconies of red velvet, women of forged iron.

6. Márgara and Vanessa

The first time that a man sees Márgara the Beauty naked, he is blinded forever. The second time, he loses his four wisdom teeth.

The first time that a man sleeps with the Beauty Vanessa, he loses his four wisdom teeth; the second time, his appendix comes out his belly button; the third time, he grows ten hairs on the sole of his left foot. But, the fourth time, his migraines disappear forever. Some prefer to begin directly with the fourth time, everything has its price.

7. The Blondest

The Blondest has a son who is a boy both iridescent

and ephemeral. She was raped, as the story goes, by an earthworm that must have waited for her on a solitary path, binding her plump legs with its thin body, like a legless lasso, made of nothing but will and rope. Others say it was her brother-in-law. Others say her brother-in-law is an earthworm.

8. Tradition
A reputable European brothel of the nineteenth century needed to have a fat girl, a skinny girl, a Jewish girl, and a black girl. The Jewish girl could also be the skinny girl, but not the fat girl.

9. Foreign Delegations
Great is the House, great is its fame. At times, it receives delegations from foreign lands, like that group of zombies traveling all around America, showing their death certificates at all the brothels (but no one believes them, they're poor, they're Haitians, they're dead) to prove that they didn't die of AIDS.

10. A Woman
At the door of the brothel, a man announces the merchandise to the passersby. He offers them a woman who is very white but covered with moles and another given to fantasies of the flesh and another with eyes like swords and another capable of playing three instruments in unison and another that roars like the rotor of a runaway helicopter and another from a foreign country and another who forgets her own name at every turn of her sex. Nevertheless, inside there is only one woman. Nevertheless, the man isn't lying.

11. Disloyalty

No one speaks well of Lina, of her company, of her loyalty, of her tastes. There were some clients who didn't want to enter her for fear of running into a creditor.

12. Multitudes

The House is enormous; its fame is enormous. On the eves of holidays, a multitude exhausts its boarders. On the ground floor there is a first-aid station; there are bathrooms everywhere; on the third floor, a buffet and a small morgue sharing a freezer. People are careless and ignore the waste baskets. Working nonstop, the skilled personnel carefully separate out the fulfilled fantasies and quickly sweep up the frustrated desires.

13. Joys and Disappointments

The disappointment of someone who is loved by a real nurse disguised for that purpose as a prostitute.

For those who wish to experience strong emotions, we propose coupling while skydiving, a horde of rats, or incest.

14. Repository of Fantasies

The fantasies offered to clients of little imagination are provided by other clients who, after fulfilling them, no longer are able to or want to keep them as fantasies. They serve, more than anything, as advertising for the House, as each one of them is visible proof that a client has walked away satisfied.

7

Faith

Orders Are Orders

I'm just the Executor. The ones who are really responsible, the ones who give the orders, are Higher Up. He kept giving that phrase as an excuse when, some time after finishing His Work in six days, the first souls to get their reward began to ascend, complaining about the gross errors of Creation.

Cast Out

You have disobeyed my commandment, said the Lord to Adam and Eve. And, not giving them another chance, he promptly woke them up.

Wrestling with the Angel

What a disgrace to think you've wrestled with the Angel and to discover, looking at the corpse, that you've just beaten a mugger. For this reason it's better to not resist so much, to maintain the illusion, to be defeated.

The Angel of Death

The Lord of the Mansion has sent me to you: I am the Destroyer of Joys and He Who Disperses All Gatherings. Thus spoke Azrael, the Angel of Death, to the unlucky king.

The king then begged for one more day, to return the stolen riches he kept in his treasury, and not to have this debit charged to the account of his evil works. But the angel announced, with frightening voice, that the days of his life were numbered and his breaths counted and his moments written down. And the king then asked for just one more hour: and even this hour, said the angel, was already included in the accounting, and his fate was written and must be fulfilled in that instant. And the angel took the king's soul, and the king rolled off his throne and fell dead.

And behold men wonder: if the exact instant of his death was written, signed, and sealed, why or for what purpose did the angel pause to have a vain argument?

And Someone responds: it was so that this story could be told.

Rabbi versus Angel

A Hasidic rabbi promises one of his disciples that he will save his suffering wife by doing no more than praying for her.

Days later, the weeping disciple confronts him: his wife has died.

"It's not possible," the rabbi assures him. "While I prayed, I managed to take away the sword from the Angel of Death."

"My wife is dead and buried," insists the young man.

The rabbi meditates for a moment, trying to understand.

"There's one other possibility: perhaps when he realized he was missing his sword, the angel decided to strangle her with his bare hands."

The curious thing is that this brief history has been compiled by Nathan Ausubel, the unbeliever, in a collection of humorous stories.

The Irresistible Cry

The cry of the Exterminating Angel is so shrill and frightening that no one can resist it. Two young men tried to resist it using Ulysses's method, with wax in their ears; but the cry penetrated the other orifices of their bodies, making them explode. An old woman tried to resist it by seeking refuge in her senile indifference; but the cry destroyed her indifference, did away with her senility, and the old woman died converted into an intense twenty-three-year-old. The Exterminating Angel himself tried to resist it and lost almost all the feathers from his wings and lost his wrath and his voice and forever lost his desire to cry out, and ever since then the Apocalypse is impossible.

Repression

In hell repression is firm but necessary: the constant rebellion of its inhabitants is barely controlled. The terrible, crushing resignation of paradise, however, more closely resembles death.

Mistaken Copyist

The acrobat blows fire through his nostrils and the clowns
run each other through with swords and the elephants have
their trunks stopped up with acrylic plugs and the lions vomit
up the magician's head and if tradition mentions circles, it's
perhaps through the error of some copyist: it's in nine *cir-
cuses* (a single Ringmaster with his pitchfork) that we will
be punished.

Rumors

It is said that the devil tends to adopt the form of a male goat or a great black dog. It is also said that a strong sulfur smell tends to precede his apparition. It is said that even in his human form he tends to wear a long tail and cloven hoofs. The inhabitants of the Earth tend to spread these and other comforting rumors, looking at their feet with great relief.

Witch Cats

The Inquisition tries the cats for witchcraft and condemns them to be burned. Thus, free from predators, the rats multiply and spread the plague. The death that ensues makes the inquisitors more prudent in the face of an enemy that's too powerful. Thus, free from predators, we cats multiply so we can continue serving the Lord of Hell.

The Old Devil

The devil appeared to a man without goat legs, without beard or tail, without a pitchfork or anything else; but he knew it was the devil because it had the face of the vice principal of Washington Middle School, School District 7, when she had been drinking wine at lunch or was on a diet.

The Fervent Atheist

A man practiced an almost mystical atheism. He fervently believed in the harmfulness of belief in the supernatural. Nevertheless, he never allowed his children to open umbrellas in his house or to say the word "death" aloud, but not out of faith, just good manners and prudence. Death came just the same; it doesn't need to be called.

The Reward

There's a cure for everything, except death, insisted the good man all his life. And he was so good that the Judges chose to not grant him reincarnation and thereby not disillusion or make a liar out of him.

Suicide

The misfortune of the suicide: to leap into the void at the precise instant in which it begins to be filled, to be filled slowly and without recourse.

Hermit I

With ambrosia at the table of the kings was the hermit tempted, and with the smell of the dark bread that his mother took out of the oven in the morning. And ten years he resisted and afterward was free of the temptation.

With the fears and horrors of hell was the hermit tempted, and with the image of his very own stepfather, reins in hand. And fifteen years he resisted and was free of the temptation.

With women abounding in flesh and desires was the hermit tempted, and with the daughter of the village blacksmith, who had once smiled at him. And twenty years he resisted and was free of the temptation.

And after twenty years of life in the desert, now nothing tempted him, and his heart was parched and dry, and his sacrifice was now worthless.

Hermit III

To be a hermit, said the hermit, you don't need physical solitude. Even in a bustling crowd an authentic hermit can seek refuge in his interior hermitage. One New Year's Eve, while the rest of the guests were eating sugared almonds and crying and fighting, the hermit went to his interior refuge and found it occupied. There were two of them; they were naked and drinking cider. They invited him in.

Hermit IV

When there are no temptations, the hermit gets bored. He's not always bathed in Grace, not always approaching the Light. Sometimes he's sitting on a rock by the hermitage door, and he watches the shape of the clouds and thinks that he wasted the years of his life resisting every pleasure and happiness, and he thinks that he was also useless (not even in the way of the lilies of the field) for making others happy. (The lilies of the field are beautiful and fragrant and the hermit is old and dirty.) And then he has a great urge to weep; but he resists it, because that is the supreme temptation and also because resisting is the only thing he's learned to do really well and thus, in passing, occupies himself.

Master and Friend

You must find your place, the only one made for your body, the place where your mind and stomach and each one of your cells feel safe, protected, and at peace, the only place inaccessible to your enemies, says the Master. The disciple searches all night: all of the patio's tiles look alike, indifferent. Toward morning, exhausted, he falls asleep in a corner. Waking up, he recalls his failure. You won, says the Master: for you never could have fallen asleep in a place that was not yours. The disciple notices that his wallet is missing. I have taken it, says the Master. But am I perchance your enemy?

Lotus

Sitting for hours in the lotus position, repeating the mantra that will bring enlightenment to his spirit, and enlightenment comes late or comes to someone else, or it comes just when (but just for an instant) he's left, or it comes—precisely from having waited too long—in such an unforeseen form that it's not possible to hold on to it, prove it, or show it.

Turtles

Seven turtles hold up the world. This condition that was so evident a few millennia ago is now difficult to prove. They're invisible and they're gigantic. Their enormous mass attracts our planet, forcing it to lean against their shells. Unbelievers ask about the points of contact. I don't have to answer them: one of the seven turtles is about to die. You always want what you can't have.

Ingram Content Group UK Ltd.
Milton Keynes UK
UKHW021528250423
420618UK00021B/349